llama llama

family vacation

Anna Dewdney

family vacation

Based on the bestselling children's book series by Anna Dewdney

PENGUIN YOUNG READERS LICENSES
An Imprint of Penguin Random House LLC, New York

ISBN 9780593097120

Llama Llama and Mama Llama are relaxing on the front porch.

Llama Llama circles a date on the calendar.

"One day until we go away!" Llama Llama says.

"That's right," Mama Llama responds. "Our first vacation together."

"But we can't just drive to Sandy Island," says Mama Llama. "We have to take a plane and then a boat."

Llama Llama has never flown in a plane before. "It'll be a fun adventure together, Llama," Mama says.

Grandma Llama joins them on the porch. She's excited for the vacation, too!

Just then, Nelly Gnu rolls past on her skateboard.

"Hello, everyone!" Nelly Gnu says.

Llama Llama tells Nelly Gnu about his vacation plans.

"I've never flown in a plane, either," Nelly says. "I bet it's like jumping on a trampoline!"

"So many new things," Llama Llama says. "First vacation, first time on a plane, first time meeting new cousins!" Llama Llama is very nervous.

"You know," Grandma Llama says, "when your Mama was your age, she got a little nervous before traveling. I gave her a photo diary to keep track of all her new experiences."

"I still have it!" Mama Llama replies.

"I know—I'll keep a diary of my own!" Llama Llama says. "I can take all the same photos Mama took as a kid."

"That's a great idea," Grandma Llama replies. "You can borrow my camera!" Nelly Gnu adds.

Upstairs, Mama Llama and Nelly Gnu help Llama Llama prepare for the trip.

"This can be the first photo in your vacation diary," Nelly Gnu says, and she snaps a photo of him. "Llama Llama packs his suitcase."

The next morning, it's time to leave for vacation. "Next stop: airport!" Mama Llama says.

After going through security, Llama Llama takes his seat on the plane.

"Are you nervous, Mama?" he asks.

"No, I'm excited," Mama Llama responds. "And you should be, too."

Once the flight attendant explains the safety instructions, the plane takes off.

"Wow, the houses and cars look like toys from up here!" Llama Llama says.

Llama Llama takes more photos to add to his travel diary. Before he knows it, the plane lands.

"You were right, Mama," he says. "Flying *was* a fun new experience."

After a short car ride, Llama Llama meets Cousin Llama and
Libby Llama for the first time.

"It's been way too long!" Cousin Llama says as he hugs
Mama Llama.

Together, the Llama family boards a boat to Sandy Island. Grandma Llama loves the smell of the fresh ocean air. Once they reach the shore, Cousin Llama takes them to the house.

"It's just the same as I remember it," says Mama Llama.

Libby shows Llama Llama
around town on their scooters.
Sandy Island is much smaller than
Llama Llama's neighborhood.
The main street has only four stores!
Llama Llama makes sure to take lots
of photos for his vacation diary.

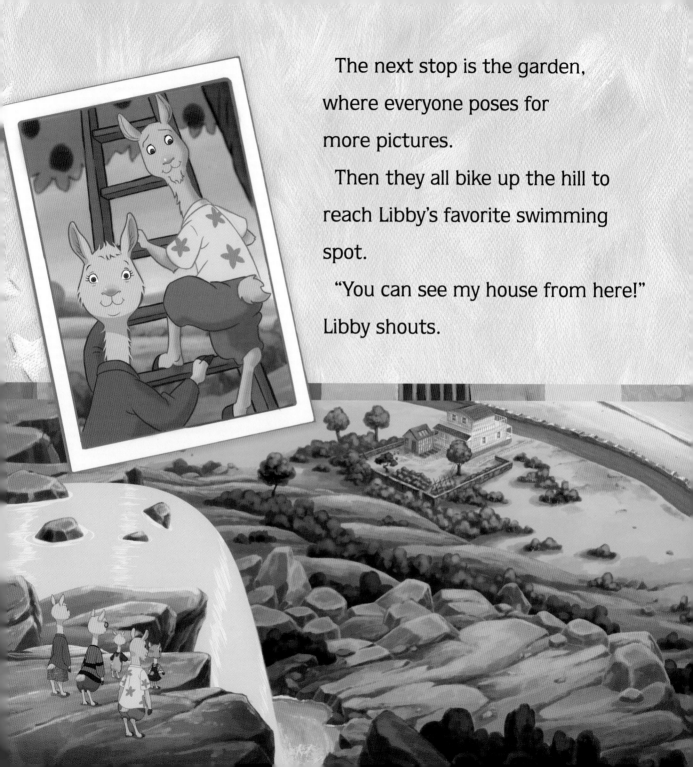

The next stop is the garden, where everyone poses for more pictures.

Then they all bike up the hill to reach Libby's favorite swimming spot.

"You can see my house from here!" Libby shouts.

Llama Llama dives into the chilly water.

"I can see why they call it Cold Pond," he says with a shiver.

"Your Mama has a photo of the pond in her travel diary," Libby says. "You have to take one, too, Llama Llama!"

That night, Cousin Llama and Libby prepare dinner for the whole family.

The food is delicious, but Llama Llama is very tired after such an adventurous day.

Llama Llama and Libby climb into hammocks on the porch, just like the ones Mama Llama and Cousin Llama used to sleep in when they were kids.

"Whoa, it *really* swings," Llama Llama says.

"Don't worry, it barely moves when you're asleep," Libby says.

Llama Llama and Libby say good night to the birds in the tree and drift off to sleep in their hammocks.

The next morning,
Grandma Llama makes
pancakes on a stick to eat
at the beach.

"Another first, right,
Llama Llama?" Libby asks.

Llama Llama snaps a photo for his travel diary.

"Just like the ones we used to eat as kids!"
says Cousin Llama.

Libby and Llama Llama collect seashells on the beach. When they put the shells to their ears, they can hear the sound of ocean waves.

"I think you've got most of the pictures your Mama has in her photo diary, Llama," Libby says. "But you still have to see Drippy Tunnel!"

Llama Llama has never been anywhere like Drippy Tunnel before.

"Wow," Llama Llama says. "Are you sure it's okay for us to be in here?"

"It sure is," Cousin Llama responds. "Just watch out for the drips!"

Libby reminds Llama Llama to take a photo for his diary.

The Llama family celebrates another full day with dinner on the porch.

"I wish island time was all the time," says Llama Llama before he goes to sleep in the hammock again.